# SOCCER
## with Mom

## By Frank J. Berrios • Illustrated by Jess Golden

A GOLDEN BOOK • NEW YORK

Text copyright © 2016 by Frank J. Berrios
Illustrations copyright © 2016 Jess Golden
All rights reserved. Published in the United States by Golden Books, an imprint of Random House Children's Books, a division of Penguin Random House LLC, 1745 Broadway, New York, NY 10019, and in Canada by Random House of Canada, a division of Penguin Random House Ltd., Toronto. Golden Books, A Golden Book, A Little Golden Book, the G colophon, and the distinctive gold spine are registered trademarks of Penguin Random House LLC.
randomhousekids.com
Educators and librarians, for a variety of teaching tools, visit us at
RHTeachersLibrarians.com
Library of Congress Control Number: 2014957499
ISBN 978-0-553-53854-0 (trade) — ISBN 978-0-553-53855-7 (ebook)
Printed in the United States of America
10 9 8 7 6 5 4 3 2 1

**T**oday is Saturday—the day of our big soccer match!

"Let's go, Mikey!" says my mom. "Time to fuel up with a good breakfast."

Mom is the coach of our soccer team, the Blue Bisons. At soccer practice and games, my sister and I call her Coach Karen, just like the other kids do.

After breakfast, we pile into the car
to get some of our teammates.

"Thanks for picking us up, Coach Karen,"
says Drew.

We unload the car, then head over to the bench on our side of the field. We bring a few extra soccer balls for warm-ups, and lots of water.

"Okay, team, time to warm up!"
says Coach Karen.

First we do thirty seconds
of toe-touches.

Then we
jog in place.

Warm-ups loosen our muscles so we
don't get hurt while we're running around.

"Now let's do some dribbling and passing drills," says Coach Karen.

Dribbling means kicking the ball in front of you while you run.

Dribbling and passing a soccer ball take lots of practice!

Soccer is pretty simple. There are eleven players on each team. Ten of them, called field players, run around the field and try to kick the ball into the other team's goal. I'm a field player.

The eleventh player is the goalie, who protects the net at all times. My big sis, Jen, is our goalie. Goalies are the only players who can use their hands during the game.

Field players can never touch the ball with their hands. They have to use their feet to dribble, pass, or try to score. They can use their head or chest to hit the ball.

The team that scores the most goals before the end of the match wins!

Now it's time to play soccer!
Our team starts the game on defense.
That means we need to stop the Green
Dragons from getting the ball in our goal.

One of the Dragons strikes the ball toward our goal, but my sister catches it! She's a great goalie.

Now we have the ball, and it's our turn
to play offense.

Kevin is one of our fastest players. Once he gets the ball, he quickly dribbles past two of the Green Dragons' defenders—and kicks the ball past their goalie!

Our team scores the first goal!

# Go, Bisons!

"Great teamwork!" calls Coach Karen.

Halftime gives us a chance to rest, drink some water, and go over the game plan.

"Good job out there, Bisons!" says Coach Karen. "Remember to pass and move. Work together to get the ball down the field."

After halftime, the Green Dragons start to play much better! They pass the ball back and forth while we try to stop them.

One of their best players scores!
Now the game is tied!

In soccer, we run, kick, jump, and spin—and sometimes we stumble and fall down. But we always have fun!

Just before time runs out, we score a goal—and win! But whether we win or lose, we always congratulate the other team on a game well played. That's called good sportsmanship.

Everyone thinks Mom is a great coach. "Thanks, Coach Karen! See you next week!" say our teammates.

# We love soccer— and our soccer coach mom!